This book belongs to

S Y

_____

Old Mother Turtle
and the Three Frogs

by
K.B. Austin

Illustrated by
MANDA PIE

Dream ✦ Star
TULSA, OKLAHOMA

Published by Dream Star Productions.
Dream Star Productions ▪ 4306 South Peoria, Suite 705 ▪ Tulsa, OK 74105 ▪ (918) 744-6645

Library of Congress Control Number: 2005934559

Old mother turtle and the three frogs/by K.B. Austin,
illustrated by Manda Pie

Summary: Three little frogs come to discover their true natures
through the inspired and creative efforts of a wise, old mother turtle.

ISBN 0-9772027-0-4 (Hardcover)

Manufactured in United States
Printed by The Covington Group, Kansas City, Missouri
Prepress production by Protype, Inc., Tulsa, Oklahoma

ACKNOWLEDGMENTS:

I offer my deepest and most heartfelt thanks and yippees to:
my children, Jeremy and Kobi, you never tired of my stories
and just kept asking for more; Manda and Karenna, my dear
sisters in spirit, illustrator and graphic artist extraordinaire,
you just kept the magic coming; my fabulous "Dream Team,"
Cheryl Northness, Michael Gibson, Mary Duncan and David
Rechter for hours of dedication and limitless support; Joan
Crager for her empowering invitation that once more set all in
motion; my many generous benefactors; and B.J. Dohrmann and
the magnificent IBI Global family, who honored and believed
in me and my dream. You've all contributed generously and
unceasingly. Thank you, dear ones. This book would not have
been possible without you!

A portion of the proceeds from this book will be donated to The Results
Project and MannaRelief, nonprofit organizations dedicated to the health
and well-being of children around the world.

To my son, Jeremy,
for whom this story came.

Old Mother Turtle sat on her favorite log *humphing* and *tisking, tisking* and *humphing.* She tapped her tail and nodded her head in time with her thoughts. In all her years she had never seen her pond in such a state of disharmony. And all because of three little frogs. Something had to be done . . . quickly!

These three little frogs were constantly *huffing* and *puffing* about themselves, never giving anyone in the pond a moment's peace. They were continually *boasting* and *gloating, gloating* and *boasting.* Everyone in the pond was sick of them!

The other frogs complained bitterly about their behavior. The dragonflies avoided them. The fish swam away in disgust. Even the birds flew to the other end of the pond to get a drink.

No one wanted to see or hear them anymore!

6

Their boasting and gloating rang out over the pond. "I'm older and bigger and smarter than you are," said the first little frog to the second little frog. Then he puffed himself up as big as he could and hopped around *boasting* and *gloating, gloating* and *boasting.*

"Oh yeah," replied the second little frog. "We all hatched at the same time. You should know that! I guess that makes me smarter than you. In fact, that makes me the smartest frog in this pond!" Then he began to strut around with a big smug look on his face *huffing* and *puffing, puffing* and *huffing.*

The third little frog piped in, "Get lost! Who wants to listen to you two? Nobody dares come near me. I'm the biggest . . . and the smartest . . . and the bravest frog in this pond!" Then he stuck his tongue out and, to prove his point, triumphantly snatched in a fly, *grumphing* and *humphing, humphing* and *grumphing.*

And so it went all day long, day after day, night after night.

ld Mother Turtle sighed heavily. She positioned herself more securely on her log, cleared her throat, stretched out her neck, and looked toward the sun. This always helped her to think more clearly during a state of emergency.

Suddenly, she sneezed with a tremendous blast!

Inspiration had struck!

"Haaa

She remembered that about this time every year, two little children would come down to the pond every day to swim and play. They brought buckets, shovels, rafts and inner tubes. The little girl had a big round raft that looked just like a giant frog with a crown on its head. Perfect!

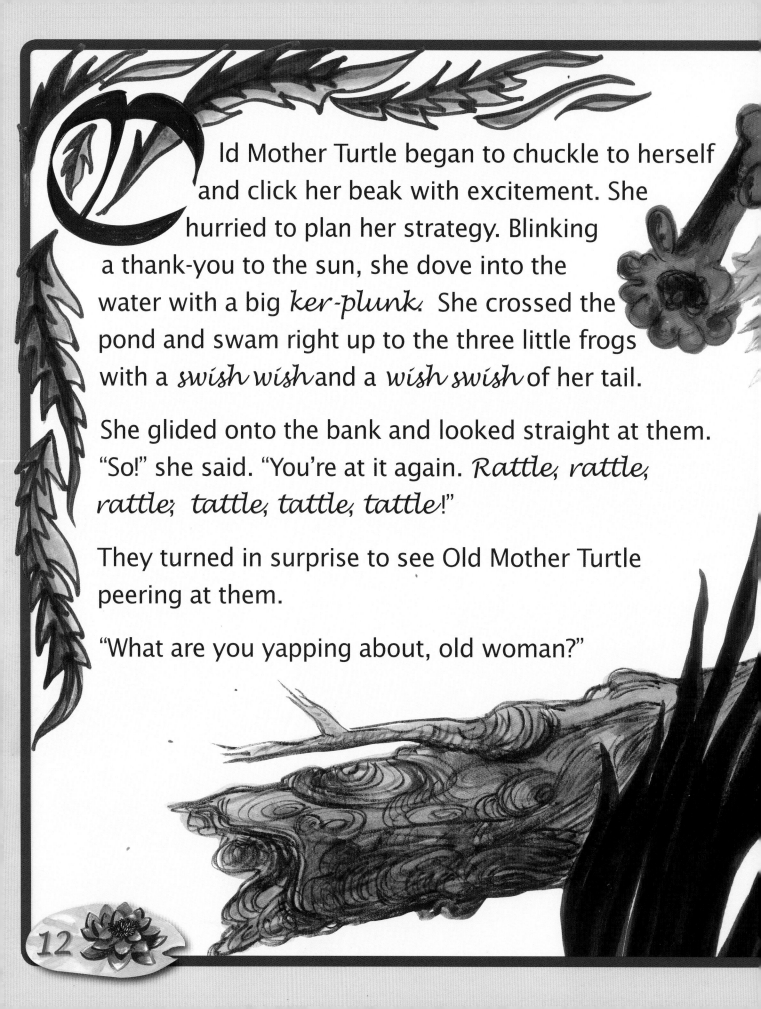

ld Mother Turtle began to chuckle to herself and click her beak with excitement. She hurried to plan her strategy. Blinking a thank-you to the sun, she dove into the water with a big *ker-plunk.* She crossed the pond and swam right up to the three little frogs with a *swish wish* and a *wish swish* of her tail.

She glided onto the bank and looked straight at them. "So!" she said. "You're at it again. *Rattle, rattle, rattle; tattle, tattle, tattle!*"

They turned in surprise to see Old Mother Turtle peering at them.

"What are you yapping about, old woman?"

"Get lost!"

"Yeah, go away!" they yelled.

"*Humph*," grunted Old Mother Turtle in disgust. She glared long and hard at them. "All right, I'll do that," she said. "But don't say I didn't warn you. When King Bravado comes to take you away . . . down, down, down deep to the bottom of the pond, don't blame me." She turned as if to swim away.

"Stop!" "What?" "Wait!"

they shouted in unison.

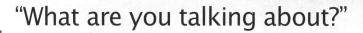

"Come back here!"

"What are you talking about?"

"Who's King Bravado?" they croaked.

"You've never heard of King Bravado?," snapped Old Mother Turtle. "Why, he's the Frog King of this pond."

"Frog King!"

"Frog King!"

"Frog King!" exclaimed each of the three frogs one after the other. You've got to be kidding!"

They all began to laugh uncontrollably.

The first little frog laughed so hard he rolled right off his lily pad into the water with a big *klunk plunk*. Up he popped with a *zat splat* and said, "You've been sitting in the sun too long, old woman. A Frog King in this pond? Huh!" Then off he swam *giggling* and *wiggling, wiggling* and *giggling* to himself.

The second little frog was swimming around in circles clutching his puffed-up belly, trying to catch his breath.

He finally slowed down enough to say, "*Fooey shooey*, Old Mother Turtle. It sounds like you're up to a whopper of a whale tale to me. Either that or a crack in your shell is causing your brain to swell!" Off he went in circles again, *cackling* and *gackling, gackling* and *cackling.*

The third little frog had laughed so hard that he had gotten the hiccoughs. He was on the bank *hopping* and *flopping, flopping* and *hopping* with each *hick huck* ! He looked like a giant green jumping bean. He finally settled down enough to say, "That's the funniest thing I've ever heard! Why, he must be such a great king that he's a secret! So scary that nobody has ever seen him except you, old woman. What's he going to do? Come out one night and eat us for supper? *Gulp gulp, slurp slurp?*"

"No," replied Old Mother Turtle calmly. "He won't eat you . . . he'll just take you way down deep to the bottom of the pond, *badaloop, dadaloop, badaloop,* and make you eat your words, *garoop, garoop.*"

Whooping and *hollering, hollering* and *whooping,* the three frogs yelled out one after the other.

"Eat our words!"

"Oh, that's funny, that's really funny!"

"Sure, sure. Eat our words. How's he going to do that?"

Old Mother Turtle crouched down low on the bank, digging her claws into the dirt for effect. She squinted her eyes and peered sharply at each of the little frogs. Holding their gaze for a long moment, she said, "It's easy. If what you say is true, then you float right up to the top. But if what you say is not, then . . . *bop, zop,* you sink quicker than a *wink . . . plink, dink.*"

our words catch in your throat and roll down into your belly and stick like *yuck muck* from a *glop swamp*. You'd be stuck in the *icky sticky, sticky icky* goo of what you've said that isn't true. You'd never come up!"

he three little frogs shivered. They began to feel a little frightened and wondered if Old Mother Turtle's story could really be true!

One little frog shook himself, gathered his courage, stood his ground and shouted, "*Riddle dee, fiddle dee, diddle dee dee,* you don't scare me! Why even if there were such a king, we're too smart for him. He'd never catch us. So hush!"

"Don't be so sure of that," said Old Mother Turtle. "Wherever you go, he knows. Whatever you say, he hears. Whatever you do, he sees. He always wins. Your only way out is to tell the truth. Then he'd let you go free."

"Enough of your *silly sally, willy wally* talk," screamed another little frog. "I can say anything I want! And whatever I say can't hurt me!"

"Now listen here, you pesky little pollywogs," snapped Old Mother Turtle. "You can't be you if what you say isn't true. Your words have got to match what you do!"

"There she goes again!" yelled the last little frog.

"Take your rhymes and riddles somewhere else. We don't want you here. Go away!"

Old Mother Turtle smiled to herself, turned and swam away, leaving the three little frogs *hooting* and *hollering, hollering* and *hooting.*

22

The day finally came.
The children arrived.

ld Mother Turtle watched the little girl and boy come down the hill and cross the meadow, dragging their rafts behind them. She waited patiently all day while they swam and played. Late in the afternoon she saw her chance. The little girl went to shore, leaving her raft floating off behind her.

The wind began to blow it across the pond, over toward the cattail rushes where Old Mother Turtle was hiding. She swam over to it, took the string in her beak and pulled it slowly, deep into the heart of her hideaway. She swam back out, climbed up onto her favorite log and waited.

Long after the children had left and just as the sun began to set, Old Mother Turtle swam over to the three little frogs with a *swoosh woosh,* and a *woosh swoosh* of her tail to give them one last warning. They sneered and jeered, refusing to take her seriously, convinced that there was no King Bravado. Old Mother Turtle swam away, certain that her plan would work.

here was a full moon that night. Old Mother Turtle coasted quietly into the cattails and pulled the raft out into the open so that it glowed in the moonlight against the dark shadows of the rushes. She positioned herself and waited for the three little frogs to come out and play. Soon she could hear their loud voices echoing over the pond, their *whooping* and *hollering, hollering* and *whooping* ringing out into the night.

In a low, deep, resounding voice she began to speak.

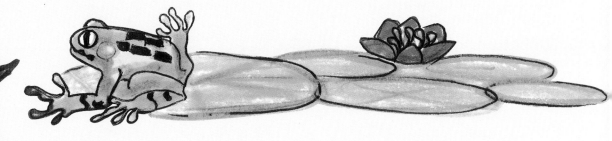

Silence! Silence, I say! I am King Bravado. I have come for the weighing of your words!"

The three little frogs could not believe their ears. For the first time in their lives, they were speechless. They peered through the pond's murky shadows toward the sound of the voice. There in the moonlight, crown gleaming, they spied the giant frog. King Bravado! They shook with fear. Old Mother Turtle's words came back to them. She had been right! They huddled close together *shivering* and *quivering, quivering* and *shivering.*

The voice of King Bravado rang out again.

"*Hacklers* and *cacklers, boasters* and *gloaters*... I command you. Come forward! Each of you, one by one, until I am done!"

The three little frogs stared at each other in terror, their eyes as round as saucers. Their bodies cold as ice. Their hearts pounded, "Ba Boom, Ba Boom," like drums beating out their thoughts. "We're doomed, we're doomed." They tried to speak. Nothing happened. They tried to swallow. Fear stuck in their throats. No words would come out. Everything was beginning to happen just as Old Mother Turtle said it would. They became even more frightened.

Once again, King Bravado's voice bellowed out over the water, interrupting their thoughts.

"Do you think I do not know where you are? That I cannot see you frightened over there on the bank, scrunched together like sardines? I see you *shuddering* and *shaking, quivering* and *quaking.* A pitiful sight you are indeed! Where are your brave words now when you need them?"

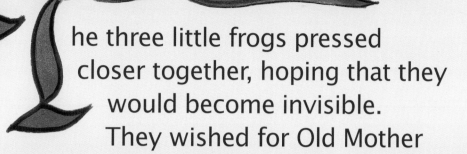

The three little frogs pressed closer together, hoping that they would become invisible.

They wished for Old Mother Turtle's presence. They began to wish for all kinds of things. Wings to fly away to safety. The ability to vanish into thin air. Magic powers to erase their past words. A frog hero to save them. In short . . . a miracle.

It came. And of all places, from King Bravado himself!

His voice boomed out louder than ever. "Listen well, oh you boasters! Your fears have made you tiny indeed . . . but perhaps there is yet hope for you. Let it not be said that I am without mercy for ones so young. I will give you one last chance."

A seed of hope began to sprout in the hearts of the little frogs. They peered across the water, staring intently at the king.

He gave a royal command.

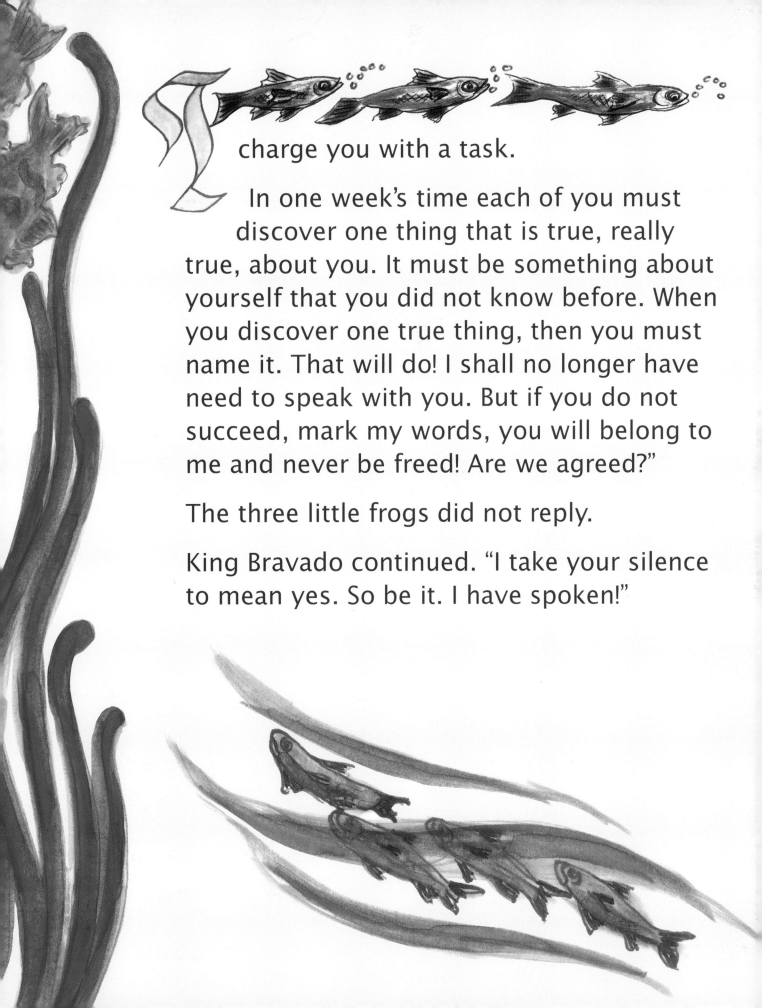

charge you with a task.

In one week's time each of you must discover one thing that is true, really true, about you. It must be something about yourself that you did not know before. When you discover one true thing, then you must name it. That will do! I shall no longer have need to speak with you. But if you do not succeed, mark my words, you will belong to me and never be freed! Are we agreed?"

The three little frogs did not reply.

King Bravado continued. "I take your silence to mean yes. So be it. I have spoken!"

With these final words, Old Mother Turtle reached down under the raft, found the air plug, and released it. The raft slowly began to sink beneath the water, *bloop bloop bloop, blup blup blup*, until it completely disappeared from sight, leaving only a stream of bubbles.

As the little frogs sat watching, it seemed as if King Bravado had slowly and majestically vanished beneath the surface to return to his throne deep at the bottom of the pond.

They were dazed. They could not believe their good fortune. As they looked at one another with relief, they knew that their lives would never be the same.

They *shook* and *shuddered*, *shuddered* and *shook* one last time. Exhausted, they snuggled closely together in the darkness, *huddling* and *cuddling*, *cuddling* and *huddling*, falling fast asleep.

arly the next morning, they awoke and began talking quietly about what had happened the night before. As they rehashed the night's events, pondering the task they had been given, they discovered an amazing thing. One of the little frogs could repeat everything, word for word, exactly as it had been said. He could remember the exact time, precisely where the moon had been, what the wind had been like, EVERYTHING!

His memory was spectacular!

41

The second little frog was so astounded at this discovery that he leaped way up in the air and landed with a big *thunk, plunk*! Startled, the two little frogs' mouths flew open with a loud *bop, pop*! They both stammered at the same time, "Da . . . da . . . da . . . do that again!" He promptly did and jumped even higher than before. Bewildered, the three little frogs looked at one another as if they were seeing each other for the very first time.

The third little frog said very excitedly, "Wait here while I go get Old Mother Turtle. We have to tell her what has happened. She'll know what to do!"

He darted off across the pond *dash, flash, splish, splash* and was gone from sight in an instant. The two little frogs stared after him in disbelief. When had he ever learned to swim so fast?

43

Before they could *blink* a *wink,* they saw him streaking across the pond with a *zip zap, split splat,* and he was back! Old Mother Turtle had been left far behind, swimming slowly across the pond after him.

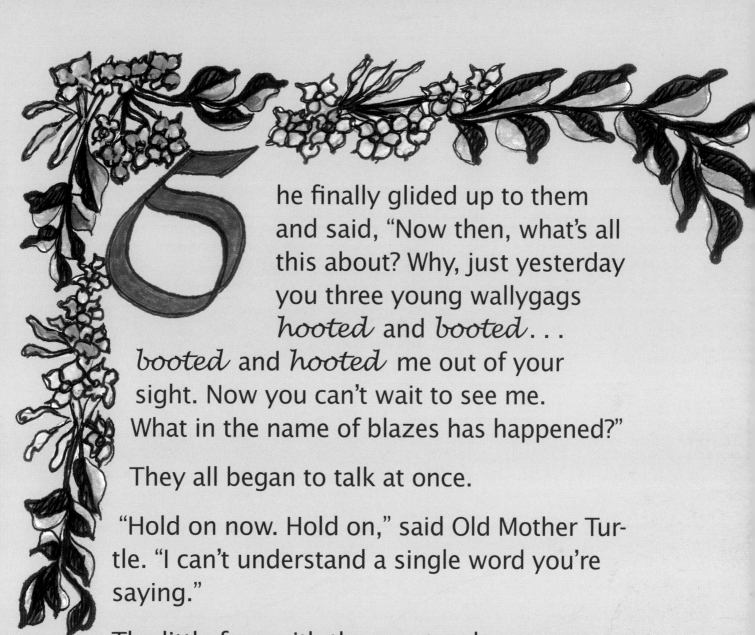

he finally glided up to them and said, "Now then, what's all this about? Why, just yesterday you three young wallygags *hooted* and *booted*... *booted* and *hooted* me out of your sight. Now you can't wait to see me. What in the name of blazes has happened?"

They all began to talk at once.

"Hold on now. Hold on," said Old Mother Turtle. "I can't understand a single word you're saying."

The little frog with the spectacular memory explained everything that had happened.

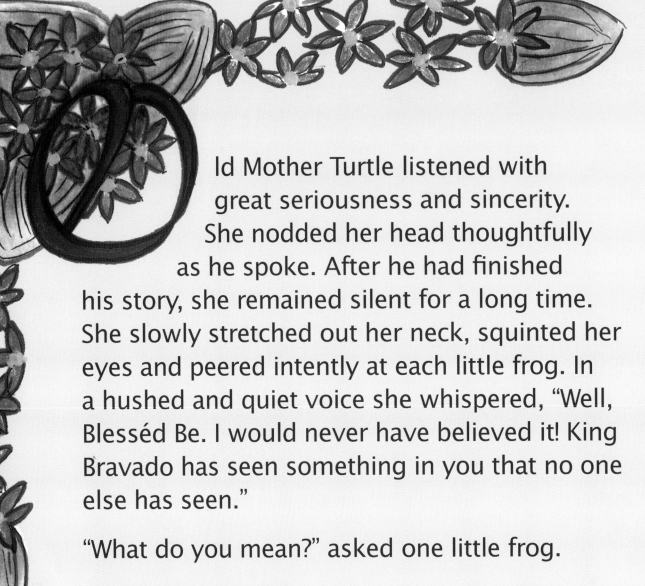

Old Mother Turtle listened with great seriousness and sincerity. She nodded her head thoughtfully as he spoke. After he had finished his story, she remained silent for a long time. She slowly stretched out her neck, squinted her eyes and peered intently at each little frog. In a hushed and quiet voice she whispered, "Well, Blesséd Be. I would never have believed it! King Bravado has seen something in you that no one else has seen."

"What do you mean?" asked one little frog.

"Huh?" said another.

"Yeah, we don't understand," said the other.

They nodded their heads in agreement.

48

"He's letting you have a second chance, isn't he? I've never known him to do that before," replied Old Mother Turtle.

"Oh!"

"Really?"

"Gosh!" gasped the three little frogs in unison.

Old Mother Turtle moved closer. She tapped her tail slowly and thoughtfully. She looked straight into the eyes of each of them. One right after the other. Her eyes began to twinkle. She smiled from ear to ear and then spoke.

"Well now, this is a very happy moment. I know what King Bravado saw."

"You do?"

"Tell us!"

"What?" they blurted out at once.

"Think about it, little ones. Think! What exactly did King Bravado ask you to do?"

To find out something about ourselves that we didn't know," volunteered the first little frog.

"Something true, really true," said the second one.

"And we had to give it a name," said the third. "And we only have a week."

"Only a week you say?" Old Mother Turtle gave a low chuckle and said, "I'll be *tithered* and *jiggered, jiggered* and *tithered!* I don't think you'll need a week!"

51

The three little frogs looked more con-fused than ever. Old Mother Turtle began to laugh big, deep, full, belly-rumbling laughs. "*Whoop whoop whoop, yooop yooop yooop.*" She laughed so hard that tears ran down into the water. *Dlink, dlink, dlink.* Then she said very affectionately, "My dears, you've just added years to my already long life. Thank you! Thank you! Thank you! Now think!"

She looked at the first little frog and said, "Remember!" At the second little frog and said, "Jump for the sky!" At the third little frog and said, "Race the wind!" She stared at them. "Think! Think! Think! You'll never sink now!"

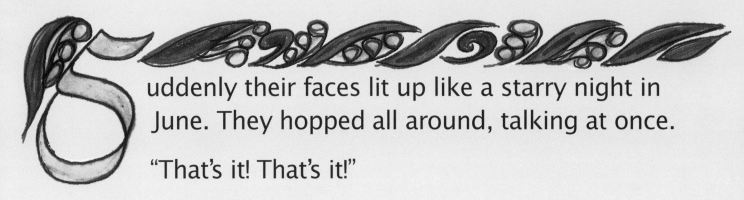

uddenly their faces lit up like a starry night in June. They hopped all around, talking at once.

"That's it! That's it!"

"I get it! I get it!"

"We did it. We did it!"

"I can remember anything! EVERYTHING!" shouted the first little frog.

"I can leap HIGH, HIGH, HIGH! Higher than the sky!" yelled the second little frog.

"I swim so fast that I go FLASH, FLASH, FLASH! And I don't even get tired!" cried the third little frog.

"You've done it!" joined in Old Mother Turtle. "You've made your discoveries in less than one day! You won't need your boasting and gloating anymore! I guess you three young whippersnappers are pretty smart after all."

"Yippee! Yippee! We're free, we're free!" chanted the three little frogs.

Old Mother Turtle continued, "So what are you waiting for? Name yourselves! Are you going to be the three little frogs forever?"

"I'm Storykeeper," said the first little frog.

"I'm Big Leaper," said the second little frog.

"I'm Flash Dasher," said the third little frog.

They hopped around laughing and hugging each other *flipping* and *flopping, flopping* and *flipping* with delight.

"*Hooray, hooray!* This is your big day!" cried Old Mother Turtle.

"Go and get yourselves ready for a big celebration. I'll alert everyone. Tonight will be a night to remember!"

Storykeeper, Big Leaper, and Flash Dasher swam off *wiggling* and *giggling, giggling* and *wiggling* with excitement.

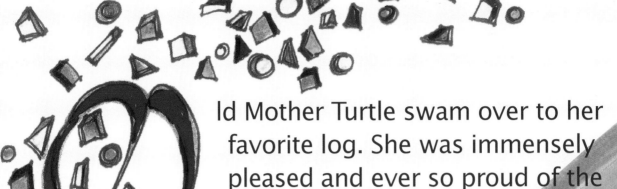

ld Mother Turtle swam over to her favorite log. She was immensely pleased and ever so proud of the three little frogs. She climbed up on her log and turned to face the sun. She listened to the sounds of harmony returning to her pond. She began to tap her tail and nod her head in time with her thoughts. Her heart was filled with peace and the joy of a whole new beginning. She sighed contentedly and began to hum to herself, "*Dum diddle dum, dum diddle dee.* Oh, what a happy day this will be!"

And indeed it was.

The end

The Author

K.B. Austin has been a storyteller since she can remember. As early as age three, she was telling improvised, animated stories to her older sister, twin brother and family pets.

She is passionate about children, health and education. K. B. is a child development and whole-brain learning specialist, has facilitated improvisational dance and drama programs for children and is currently the state director of a natural and wholistic program for children with learning and behavioral challenges. She is also a therapist, educator and public speaker.

K. B. Austin received her Masters and Doctoral degrees from the University of Massachusetts, Amherst. She currently lives in Tulsa, Oklahoma, with her two sons, Jeremy and Kobi, two Labradors and a finicky cat named Samson.

The Story

Disharmony has come to Old Mother Turtle's pond in the name of three little frogs, *boasting* and *gloating, gloating* and *boasting,* day in and day out. Their antics, lack of consideration for anyone else and their constant *huffing* and *puffing* about themselves have wreaked havoc upon all the pond dwellers. Inspired by the Sun, the help of a little girl's inner tube raft, the Moon's reflection and mythical "King Bravado," the three little frogs discover their true natures. Peace and harmony return to the pond.

ILLUSTRATOR:
Manda Pie brings her childlike spirit and lively imagination to all her creative endeavors. She is an illustrator, puppeteer and performer. She has created over one hundred original puppets, dolls and costume characters.

Her paintings, prints and performances continue to delight people of all ages.

Manda now makes her home in Tulsa, Oklahoma.

GRAPHIC DESIGNER:
Karenna LaMonica blends Old World Masters' techniques and state-of-the-art computer technology to produce inspiring paintings and illustrations. Karenna's KALM Graphics Studio of Tulsa provided the layout and design of this book.